Dear mouse friends,
Welcome to the world of

Geronimo Stilton

THE RODENT'S GAZETTE
EDITORIAL STAFF

Geronimo Stilton
A learned and brainy mouse; editor of *The Rodent's Gazette*

Thea Stilton
Geronimo's sister and special correspondent at *The Rodent's Gazette*

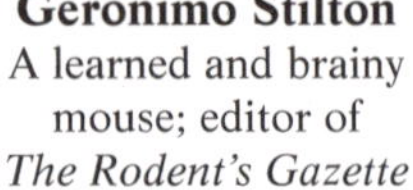

Trap Stilton
An awful joker; Geronimo's cousin and owner of the store Cheap Junk for Less

Benjamin Stilton
A sweet and loving nine-year-old mouse; Geronimo's favorite nephew

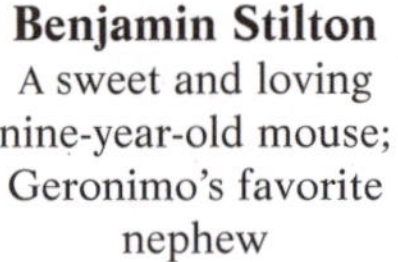

Geronimo Stilton

WELCOME TO MOLDY MANOR

Scholastic Inc.

If you purchased this book without a cover, you should be aware that this book is stolen property. It was reported as "unsold and destroyed" to the publisher, and neither the author nor the publisher has received any payment for this "stripped book."

No part of this publication may be reproduced, stored in a retrieval system, or transmitted in any form or by any means, electronic, mechanical, photocopying, recording, or otherwise, without written permission from the copyright holder. For information regarding permission, please contact: Atlantyca S.p.A., Via Leopardi 8, 20123 Milan, Italy; e-mail foreignrights@atlantyca.it, www.atlantyca.com.

ISBN 978-9-3510-3638-8

Copyright © 2013 by Edizioni Piemme S.p.A., Corso Como 15, 20154 Milan, Italy.

International Rights © Atlantyca S.p.A.

English translation © 2015 by Atlantyca S.p.A.

GERONIMO STILTON names, characters, and related indicia are copyright, trademark, and exclusive license of Atlantyca S.p.A. All rights reserved. The moral right of the author has been asserted.

Based on an original idea by Elisabetta Dami.

www.geronimostilton.com

Published by Scholastic Inc., 557 Broadway, New York, NY 10012. SCHOLASTIC and associated logos are trademarks and/or registered trademarks of Scholastic Inc.

Stilton is the name of a famous English cheese. It is a registered trademark of the Stilton Cheese Makers' Association. For more information, go to www.stiltoncheese.com.

Text by Geronimo Stilton
Original title *Una tremenda vacanza a Villa Pitocca!*
Cover by Giuseppe Ferrario (design) and Flavio Fausone (color)
Illustrations by Carolina Livio (design), Riccardo Sisti (ink), and Valentina Grassini (color)
Graphics by Chiara Cebraro

Special thanks to Beth Dunfey
Translated by Andrea Schaffer
Interior design by Kay Petronio

Printed in India by Repro India Ltd.
First printing, January 2015

Reprinted by Scholastic India Pvt. Ltd.
August 2014, October 2014

A Mouserific Birthday

My dear rodent friends, before I begin my tale, let me introduce myself. My name is Stilton, *Geronimo Stilton*, and I am the editor of *The Rodent's Gazette*, the most famouse **newspaper** on Mouse Island.

What a **story** I have for you today! It all began on a Saturday morning. But not just any Saturday — it was my BIRTHDAY!

It all began like this . . .

I absolutely adore my BIRTHDAY. I like to celebrate with my friends and receive cards and gifts. But most of all, I like to *give* presents! So I put on my **Best Suit** and got ready to go out. I was planning a FABUMOUSE party, and I wanted to get loads of surprises for all my friends.

The doorbell rang. My heart leaped as I scurried to open it. Someone had come to wish me a happy birthday!

It was my cousin Trap, who tore through my mousehole like a tornado. "Germeister, aren't you going to wish me a happy birthday? You've FORGOTTEN all about my birthday, haven't you?"

"Wh-what?" I stuttered. "Today is your BIRTHDAY? I was SURE it was next week!"

Trap began to sob like a mouseling, spraying tears everywhere. Within moments, I was soaked to the fur.

"WAAAAH! You forgot about my birthdaaaay! Gerry Berry, how could you?

I never expected this from yoooouu! No one cares about meeee!" He wiped his EYES on the sleeve of my jacket and blew his nose on my tie.

I tried to comfort him. "Trap, I am so sorry. I thought it was next week . . . Let me make it up to you. Let's celebrate together! You know, today is my BIRTHDAY, too. I was just about to go out and do a little shopping. Here's the list!"

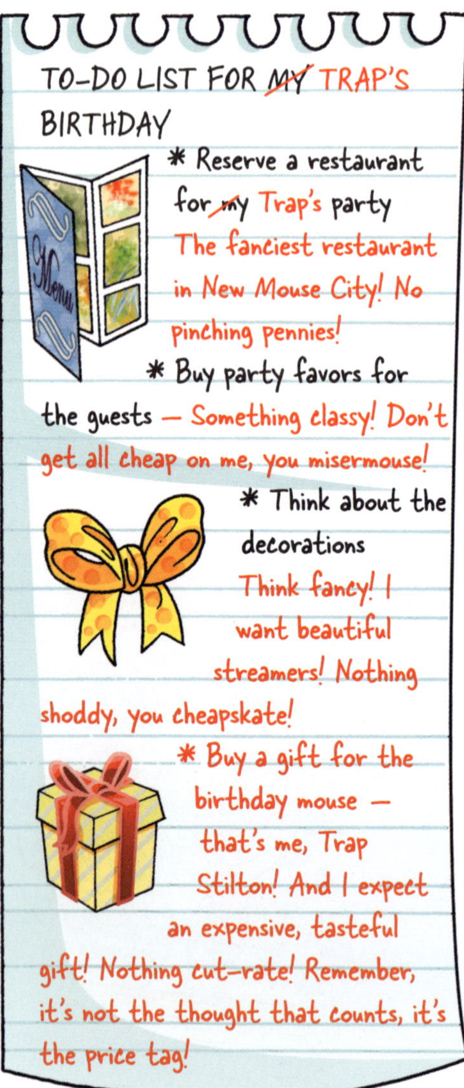

Trap immediately stopped crying. He **RIPPED** the list out of my paws and started marking it up with a *red pen*. Then he snatched my wallet and all my credit cards.

"*I'll take these!* No cheaping it up today, okay, Gerry Berry? Remember, it's my birthday. **PINCHING PENNIES** is prohibited!"

"I am not a penny-pincher!" I protested, **offended**.

"Why, I'm downright famouse for my GENEROSITY!"

For a second, I thought I saw a sly smile under Trap's whiskers. "Humph! Let me be the judge of that, Cousinkins!"

A Deal That Can't Be Missed!

As soon as we hit the streets, Trap ***raced*** ahead of me, waving my credit cards in the air. I trudged behind him, **SHOUTING**, "Trap, give them back!"

Trap scampered into the first store. I noticed there were tons of sales (fortunately for me!).

In the window, colorful banners announced a 10 PERCENT discount on shirts, a 20 PERCENT discount on jackets, a 30 PERCENT discount on jeans, a 40 PERCENT discount on ties, and a 50 PERCENT discount on boots.

"See, I'm doing you a favor," Trap told me. "Check out these sales! Think about how much you'll save on my present. This is your lucky day, Cousinkins! Now you can give me lots of presents instead of just one. Just don't be a cheapskate, okay?"

I tried to remind him that I am a generous rodent (sometimes even a little *too* generous).

But before I could squeak a word, he shoved a pair of ridiculous green boots into my paws. "Here, why don't you buy these for yourself? After all, it's your BIRTHDAY, too! Never say that I'm not generous, Cousin! Why, these are FIFTY PERCENT off. Just think about how much money you'll save!"

I wanted to say that it was easy for him to be GENEROUS with MY money! Besides, I really didn't need a pair of tacky green boots. But the salesmouse was already cooing in my ears.

"Oh, Mr. Stilton, these boots are absolutely fabumouse! They are just perfect with your outfit! You simply can't let this opportunity pass you by! Look, they're made of very shiny leather, with soft padding and a nonslip sole. The style is so *sophisticated*, all sewn by paw . . . with silver spurs and REAL gold toes!"

Green boots?

It was too bad they weren't my size. But the **SALESMOUSE** convinced me that a smaller size would be fine.

"You'll see how they stretch after a little wearing! You ab-so-lute-ly can't miss an opportunity like this!"

The salesmouse made me try them on, even though I could tell they'd be too tight. And then I couldn't remove them — they were stuck on my **PAWS**! I tried everything I could think of to **GET THEM OFF**, but nothing worked . . .

The store manager told me, "This happened once before, in 1928. There's only one solution: **Freeze your paws!**"

I've had lots of humiliating moments in my life. But putting my paws into an ice cream shop's freezer ranks among the worst!

When she **SAW** that I couldn't take off

I TRIED EVERYTHING TO GET THE BOOTS OFF MY PAWS!

I TRIED KICKING MY PAWS IN THE AIR, BUT THAT JUST MADE THE BABY POWDER FALL INTO MY SNOUT!

I TRIED ROTATING MY ANKLES, BUT I ALMOST SPRAINED THEM!

BY THE WAY, THIS WHOLE TIME, THE BOOTS WERE PINCHING MY TOES!

THE STORE MANAGER TOLD ME TO FREEZE MY PAWS. HOW HUMILIATING!

the boots, the salesmouse shrieked, "So, are you going to buy them or not?"

My ears drooped with embarrassment. But what could I do? I had to say yes! "Um, well . . . I guess I'll **buy** them. How much are they?"

When she told me the price, I thought I needed to scrape the cheese out of my ears. "*Wh-what? That much?!*"

But Trap squeaked up as if he were an official boot expert. "Listen to me! This is a real steal! These boots used to cost twice that much! Don't you realize how much you're **saving**?"

I had two choices: I could buy the **boots**, or I could cut off my paws. So I bought them, even though they were **WAY** too small!

Meanwhile, Trap was using my credit card to buy himself a **mountain** of presents. I didn't have the strength to protest: My paws hurt too much!

I tried walking on my toes, but that hurt even more. **I tried** walking on my heels, but I lost my balance and fell flat on my snout. **I tried** hopping on my left paw, then on my right, and then on both . . . but nothing worked!

Finally, I gave up. I was just destined to have **sore paws**.

Trap dragged me from one store to another. He just bought and bought and bought. Then he tried to hide how much of my money he'd spent by throwing away all the **receipts**!

TRAP'S PURCHASES

MOUSEPOD, MOUSEPAD, MOUSEPHONE — INCLUDING CASES AND BATTERY CHARGERS!

PILLOWS MADE OF FAKE CAT FUR!

FLOWERED SWIM TRUNKS!

MOUSEPHONE STAND SHAPED LIKE A WERE-CAT. SCARY!

PORTABLE FRIDGE IN THE SHAPE OF A MOUSE. IT SQUEAKS WHEN YOU OPEN IT!

PURE GOLD, DISHWASHER-SAFE SUNGLASSES!

TOOTHBRUSH HOLDERS FOR HIM AND HER!

GOLDEN EGG CUP, STUDDED WITH CRYSTALS. COMES WITH A SILVER SPOON!

SET OF PORCELAIN PLATES WITH SILVER FORKS, DESIGNED BY LOUIS MOUSON!

SPECIAL CHEESE-SCENTED, ORGANIC TOILET PAPER!

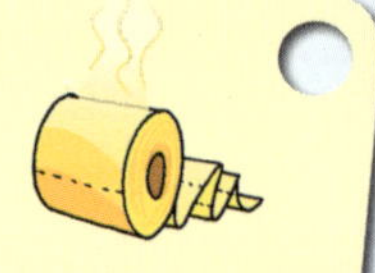

10% OFF 20% OFF 30% OFF 40% OFF

0% OFF 20% OFF 10% OFF 30% OFF 40% OFF

WATCH WITH BUILT-IN SATELLITE FEED!

GOLD LEISURE SUIT . . . BECAUSE TRAP IS WORTH IT!

TISSUE BOX COVER MADE FROM PERSIAN CAT FUR!

CAT-SHAPED USB DRIVE!

UMBRELLA THAT TURNS INTO A SHOWER!

DRESS SHIRT WITH DIAMOND BUTTONS!

LUNCH BOX THAT PLAYS THE MOUSE ISLAND NATIONAL ANTHEM!

ELEGANT HAT GUARANTEED TO GIVE THE WEARER A DISTINGUISHED AIR!

SCOTTISH KILT AND BAGPIPES!

PAJAMAS FOR EVERY DAY OF THE WEEK!

0% OFF 20% OFF 10% OFF 30% OFF 40% OFF

DINNER AT LE SQUEAKERY

Clinging to the excuse that it was his birthday, Trap kept on **BUYING**, **BUYING**, **BUYING**. Everything was on sale! Unfortunately, that meant I kept on **PAYING**, **PAYING**, **PAYING**.

Soon my cash was all gone, but Trap had conveniently remembered to bring my **checkbook**. Then I used up all my checks and was forced to use my **emergency** credit

card — the only one Trap hadn't already snatched!

All of a sudden, the **sun** was setting, and I realized I was late for my birthday dinner!

I gathered all of Trap's LITTLE packages, **MEDIUM-SIZED** packages, and **BIG** packages. There were so many of them that I had to call not **one**, not **two**, but **three**

taxis to pick them up.

Then I **RUSHED** to the restaurant where I had a reservation for dinner.

Because it was my special day, I had invited my whole family, all my friends, and all my colleagues to the most famouse, **EXPENSIVE**, and delicious restaurant in New Mouse City: *Le Squeakery*.

Still claiming that it was really *his* birthday, Trap had invited a bunch of friends, too. This dinner was going to **cost** me a tail and a paw! But a birthday comes only once a year, right? And it's so wonderful to celebrate together!

When we entered the restaurant, everyone

Saucy Le Paws

was already sitting at the table, waiting for us. **Everyone** we invited had come, and **everyone** cheered:

"Happy birthday, Geronimo! Happy birthday, Trap!"

The restaurant's famouse chef, Saucy Le Paws, came to greet us in the fur. He was a chubby mouse with a **smiley** snout and a joke always at the ready. Wiping his paws on his apron, he squeaked, "Good evening, Mr. Stilton. What can I **cook** for you tonight? Spicy Swiss pie with black

truffles, **Parmesan pie** with Russian caviar, or I also have a fresh mozzarella pie . . ."

I licked my WHISKERS. "Saucy, please make us all those wonderful pies. My friends and I will **GOBBLE** them up!"

"Yes, Saucy!" my friends cried. "Bring us the first piiiiiiee!"

We ***stuffed*** ourselves with exquisite, exclusive, and very expensive food all night long. At the end of the evening, Saucy brought out an **ENORMOUSE CAKE** covered with whipped cream, melted cheese, and tiny **CANDLES**. Trap and I blew out the candles as our friends shouted "HAPPY BIRTHDAY!"

When the bill arrived, I tried to use my credit card. But it didn't work.

How very, very strange!

"Don't worry, Mr. Stilton. You can pay me next time!" Saucy assured me. I appreciated his **KINDNESS**, but I was still very embarrassed. A Stilton always pays his debts!

Just then my grandfather William Shortpaws (also known as Cheap Mouse Willy) **took me** aside. "Grandson, why didn't your credit card work? And why did you need three **TAXIS** to carry all your packages? And why did you invite everyone you've ever met to the **MOST EXPENSIVE** restaurant in New Mouse City? And why did you let Trap bring all his friends? Today isn't his birthday — it's next week, you silly mouse! He's always playing jokes on you. You've **spent** a fortune! You've turned into a huge spender! Your success has gone straight to your snout! *Now it's up to me to put you in your place!*"

NUTTY'S DREAM

Moldy mozzarella, what a cheesebrain I'd been!

My mind was racing **FASTER** than a gerbil on a wheel. I had to talk this out with Trap.

But my cousin just laughed at me. "**Ha, ha, ha!** What, you didn't like my little joke, Germeister? What are you **COMPLAINING** about? Now you don't have to worry about shopping for my birthday! Besides, look at how much money I helped you save with all those **sales**!"

Then he pawed me one of the **packages** (that I had paid for!) and said, "Oh, and by the way, Cousinkins, here you go. **HAPPY BIRTHDAY!**"

He lowered his squeak. "It's seven pairs of pajamas, one for every day of the week. Take them — I bought the **WRONG** size!"

I took the package and went home feeling glum. What a **cheddarhead** I was!

I headed straight for bed. Unfortunately, I still couldn't get those **boots** off my paws. But I put on the pajamas that said SATURDAY, anyway.

Suddenly, the doorbell rang.

Ding-dong!

It was **NUTTY CHOCORAT**, a dear friend from my childhood.

"Geronimo, I'm so sorry I didn't make it to your party. I was working on a brand-new project that's very important, which is what brings me here tonight," he explained.

Nutty's secret chocolate stash

"Don't worry, Nutty," I assured him. "I'm **always** here for you if you need me."

"Oh, thank you, Geronimo. I knew I could count on you! Let me explain: You know that I like **chocolate** . . . "

I smiled. Everyone knew how much Nutty loved chocolate! "Of course! You are the biggest chocolate expert in New Mouse City."

"Exactly! In fact, I've recently perfected a **special formula** for new cheesy chocolates, and I want to patent the recipe. But I need some start-up money, and I don't have it. Would you be my **partner** in this new business?"

Nutty **pawed** me a cheesy chocolate to try.

"I guess I'll let my taste buds decide," I said, gobbling it up. *Yum!* I licked my WHISKERS. Holey cheese, that was the **BEST** chocolate I'd ever tasted!

"That chocolate is amazing, **NUTTY**! Of course I'll help you! How much money do you need?"

NUTTY told me the amount. It was a lot — enough to buy a lifetime supply of Cheesy Chews!

For a second, I hesitated. But I trusted my friend NUTTY and his experience as a chocolatier.

The amount Nutty needed was exactly the amount I always kept in my emergency safe — not a dollar more, not a dollar less. I opened the SAFE and gave him the entire sum. "Use this wisely, Nutty! Patent your — that is, *our* — RECIPE right away."

Nutty went away happy. "You won't regret this, Geronimo! It'll be a MOUSERIFIC success!"

The Worst Sunday of My Life!

The next day was **Sunday**. I woke up later than usual. I fixed myself **breakfast**, checked the paper for the latest news, watered the plants on my balcony, and fed my little red **fish**, Hannibal. 1

I switched on my **laptop** and went to my bank's website. Yawning, I glanced at how

1 I FED MY FISH, HANNIBAL . . .

2 I TURNED ON MY LAPTOP TO CHECK MY ACCOUNT . . .

much money was in my **ACCOUNT** . . . 2

Then I rubbed my eyes and blinked in disbelief.

"***Whaaaaaaaaaaaattt?*** There are zero dollars in my account?! **ZERO**? **ZEROOOOOOOO**?!" 3

I made it to my favorite pawchair just in time to faint. 4

CRAAAAAAAAASH!

3 THERE ARE ZERO DOLLARS IN MY ACCOUNT?!

4 I FAINTED!

When I came to, the first thing I saw was the **KIND** snout of my darling nephew Benjamin. "Uncle G, are you okay?"

I **slowly** got up. "Yes, thanks, Benjamin! I just had a nightmare. I dreamed that I had **NO MONEY** in my bank account, but that's impossible . . . "

Then my GAZE fell on the computer screen, and I saw that there was indeed NO MONEY in my bank account!

This had to be a mistake. I was about to faint again, but before I could, the door swung open, and who should storm in but Grandfather William!

"Geronimo, what happened?" he boomed.

"Grandfather, what are you doing here?" I CRIED.

"Uncle Geronimo, I was worried about you, so I called him," Benjamin squeaked.

Grandfather PATTED his little ears. "Very good, Benjamin. You knew what to do in the case of an emergency! Always call William Shortpaws! Now, Geronimo, you are paler than a slice of mozzarella. What happened? Tell me . . . and make sure it's the truth!"

Uh-oh! The last mouse I wanted to tell about my EMPTY bank account was my grandfather. (There's a reason his nickname is Cheap Mouse Willy.) By the time he stopped scolding me, it'd be time for my next birthday!

This had to be the worst Sunday of my life!

Zero? That's Impossible!

Grandfather Shortpaws stared me down like a hungry cat.

"Um, Grandfather, I, er, I checked my bank account, and . . . well, it would seem . . . that is, it looks like . . . but it must be an error!" I sputtered.

Paws quivering, I pointed at the screen. When Grandfather saw that I had no money, his fur bristled. He raised his glasses so he could scowl at me freely. "What?! You have ZERO DOLLARS in your bank account?" he yowled. "You've squandered your life savings? But how? And why?! I've been teaching you to save since you were just a wee mouseling. Why, I started telling you about the value of hard-earned money when you were in your cradle! I gave you a piggy bank shaped like CHEESE for your fifth birthday. I've been teaching you to SAVE for years! Have you learned nothing from your grandfather?"

"Grandfather, I can't explain it!" I sobbed. "I had thousands in my savings account just a day ago! I don't know how my balance can be ZERO!" I paused to think for a minute.

"Well, yesterday I did a little shopping with Trap . . . There were **sales**, and I spent all my cash. I used up all my checks, and then my credit card was declined . . . "

"So you admit it! You wasted all your money! You silly **cheese puff**!" Grandfather **barked**.

"There must be some mistake," I whispered. "I need to talk to the bank immediately, but today is Sunday, and it's **closed** till tomorrow . . . "

"Quiet! Let me think. If you keep on squeaking, I can't concentrate!" Grandfather declared. "Hmm, hmmm, hmmmm . . . "

Then he grabbed his phone and called someone.

I couldn't tell who he was squeaking with, although I did hear him grumble, "My **wasteful** grandson needs to learn a lesson, one he'll never forget! . . . Yes, a lesson on saving . . . must be made to learn the value of money . . . you think about it, since you are the experts . . . yes, I knew I could count on you!"

He hung up the phone and glared at me. "I suppose now you want to ask me for **HELP**."

"Um, yes," I admitted.

"I will help you, Geronimo, but you must do as I say, understand?" Grandfather thundered.

I hung my snout in SHAME. But I had no choice. I needed his help!

"Yes, Grandfather. I'll do whatever you tell me."

Grandfather grabbed me by the ear. "Good! Now you will leave immediately for a crash course in saving!"

"But, Grandfather . . . " I began to protest.

"No 'buts'!" he shouted. "You must leave immediately! I've arranged it all for you. If you don't learn fast, we'll be forced to sell *The Rodent's Gazette* to pay your DEBTS!"

"Sell *The Rodent's Gazette*? Never!" I yelled desperately.

"Yes, we can **sell** it to Sally Ratmousen. I'm sure she'd be interested," Grandfather replied, stroking his whiskers thoughtfully.

I pictured Sally Ratmousen, who runs *The Daily Rat*. She was my number one competitor . . . and my nemesis! She'd tap her PINK polished pawnails on *my* telephone, put her paws up on *my* desk, and boss around *my* staff, THREATENING to fire them every five minutes. Never!

"Come along now, Grandson. You're lucky I'm here to whip your finances into shape!" Grandfather scolded me.

"Okay, but where am I going?" I asked.

"There's only one rodent who can help you now: **Samuel S. Stingysnout**!"

I turned paler than a slice of Swiss cheese. Samuel S. Stingysnout is my uncle. He also happens to be the **stingiest** rodent on Mouse Island!

Grandfather William passed me his cellphone. "Here, call Uncle Samuel and squeak to him yourself!"

THE STINGYSNOUT

STINGYSNOUT FAMILY

The Stingysnouts come from the Valley of Lack. For many years, they lived at Penny Pincher Castle, their ancestral family home. Now they have relocated to Moldy Manor in the Valley of Thrift.

UNCLE SAMUEL S. STINGYSNOUT

Head of the Stingysnout family. He's always devising new ways to save!

STEVIE STINGYSNOUT

Samuel's son. When he combs his whiskers, he save the ones that fall out and uses them as dental floss!

CHINTZINA STILTON (NÉE STINGYSNOUT)

Samuel's younger sister. She is less stingy now that she has married a Stilton!

ZELDA STINGYSNOUT

Stevie's cousin. She's so stingy, she wears steel heels on her shoes so they never wear out!

FAMILY

The relationship between the Stingysnouts and the Stiltons goes back many generations, to the time when Samuel's great-grandfather married Geronimo's great-great-grandmother. Like the Stiltons, the Stingysnouts are very good-hearted. Unlike the Stiltons, they are very stingy!

THRIFTELLA AND WORTHINGTON

Twins who save money by always wearing the same clothes!

GRANDMA AND GRANDPA CHEAPERLY

Samuel's parents. They taught their children everything they know about penny-pinching!

IVY AND HOARDEN ACCOUNTS

Samuel's daughter and her husband. They save money on heat by wearing three pairs of long underwear at a time!

PENNIFORD AND SAVEANNA

Children of Hoarden and Ivy. They make their cheddar pops last for years by taking just one lick a month!

MOLDY MANOR

I gave up and said hello to **Uncle Stingysnout**.

"Nephew!" he sighed in a **TRAGIC** tone. "However did you get yourself into this mess? You've wasted all your money. What an **embarrassment** for the family! How could you? Oh, Nephew, this is just terrible. But don't worry. I'll set you back on the **narrow** road of responsibility! You will learn to **save**, if it takes the whole Stingysnout family to teach you! That's what family is for, right? By the time we're done with you, you'll be **saving** money like a stingy little squirrel! So listen up, and I'll explain how to get to Moldy Manor."

I was astonished. "**Moldy Manor?** But

doesn't the Stingysnout family live at Penny Pincher Castle?"

"No, no, we are all at Moldy Manor now. After we fixed up Penny Pincher Castle, we had to MOVE. That place was getting too *fancy*!" Uncle Samuel snorted. "Here, let me give you directions. First, you head toward the **Valley of Thrift**. Then turn down **Lack Lane** and cross over Mount Stingy. Take the turn for Lake Cheapskate. Once you pass Pinchpenny River, you'll arrive at Thrifty City. Look for Tightwad Turnpike. Turn right at Squirrel Street, and you'll find yourself at Scrooge Alley. Moldy Manor is number thirteen. I'll be expecting you!"

I hung up. I was already dreading the trip, but I had to go to Moldy Manor if I wanted

VALLEY OF THRIFT

to **save** *The Rodent's Gazette*. I didn't have a choice!

My sister, Thea, scurried in. "Geronimo, what happened? Your bank account is at **ZERO**? Didn't you keep track of how much you spent?"

"Um, y-yes," I stammered. "Well, actually, no. Trap **THREW AWAY** all my receipts . . ."

"**HERE**, I brought you something," said Thea, pawing me a red **NOTEBOOK**. "Use it to write down everything you spend.

LEARN TO KEEP TRACK OF ALL THE MONEY THAT YOU EARN AND SPEND IN A LITTLE NOTEBOOK. IT'S A GOOD HABIT!

I've been doing it for a while. It's a good habit to get into, and it's very useful for keeping your money situation UNDER CONTROL."

As my sister finished squeaking, Benjamin returned. He pawed me his piggy bank. "Don't worry, Uncle G! Here's my piggy bank. I want you to have all my savings!"

I felt my tail sag with embarrassment. I wanted to be a role model for Benjamin, and now my little nephew was looking out for me instead!

Trap followed Benjamin in.

"Germeister, what a STEW you've gotten yourself into! Now who's going to take me on vacation? Who will pay for my BIRTHDAY parties now, huh?" He sighed. "But don't worry, Gerry, we still love

Uncle G, take my savings!

you. Take this token of my affection and generosity."

He opened his **PAW** and gave me a brown jacket button.

"A brown button?" I said uncertainly. "But all my jackets are **GREEN**!"

Trap snorted. "At this point, you have **nothing**, Cousinkins! Are you really turning up your snout at my gift? Take it and say thank you!"

My fur turned redder than a cheese rind. Trap was right. I had **nothing**!

I thanked him and scurried upstairs to throw a few things in my suitcase. Then I left for **Moldy Manor**.

Welcome to Moldy Manor!

Grandfather had made all my TRAVEL arrangements at a deep discount! So instead of a half hour direct flight to Moldy Manor, it took me:

- THREE hours in a third-class train compartment 1

THREE HOURS IN A THIRD-CLASS TRAIN COMPARTMENT

SIX HOURS BY BUS

- **SIX** hours by bus 2
- **THIRTY MILES** by bike 3 — but I got a flat, so I had to ride the rest of the way in a cart full of manure 4

I had to travel the last mile by paw, and my new **boots** were pinching my **toes** like crazy!

It was **sunset** by the time I arrived at Moldy Manor. Though it was getting dark, all the lights were off.

THIRTY MILES BY BIKE

AND A RIDE ON A CART FULL OF MANURE!

The manor was a **large** building the color of stale cheese. I could tell it hadn't been painted in ages (to **save** money, naturally!). There were broken bricks and boards everywhere. Parts of the manor seemed **UNSAFE**. Uncle Samuel had posted signs that said things like GO AROUND THE BALCONIES, THEY MAY **COLLAPSE**; GO AROUND THE GUTTERS OR THEY'LL FALL ON YOUR SNOUT; and GO AROUND, OR JUST GO AWAY!

There were other **SIGNS**, too: WE DON'T BUY ANYTHING! and ABSOLUTELY NO LOANS, ESPECIALLY NOT TO FRIENDS AND FAMILY!

I looked around in the **DARK** for a doorbell, but all I found was another sign: NO DOORBELL (TO **save money** FIXING IT). GO AHEAD AND YELL; YOU'LL ONLY WASTE YOUR OWN BREATH!

GET OUT!
GO AROUND!
FALLING PLASTER!
DON'T BUY ANYTHING!
GO AROUND. BALCONIES

"Is anyone home?" I shouted.

The curtains in a first-floor window twitched. A snout with long whiskers **PEEKED** out at me. It was Uncle Samuel!

"Who is it? *Who's bothering me?* No salesmice, please. We won't buy anything!"

"It's me, Uncle Samuel! It's your nephew Geronimo!"

"*Is that you*, Geronimo?" Uncle Samuel said, squinting.

"Yes, it's me. Why is everything so dark?"

"**Nephew**, you have so much to learn." Uncle Samuel sighed. "It's to **save money**, naturally!"

I scurried to the door, but I noticed writing on the doormat: DON'T WIPE YOUR PAWS ON THE DOORMAT. YOU'LL WEAR IT OUT!

I opened the door and spotted another

message: TAKE OFF YOUR SHOES, OR YOU'LL WEAR OUT THE **FLOOR**!

I let out a low moan. I really, really wanted to take off my **boots**, but they were stuck to my paws like a glue trap!

I closed the door and stepped inside. It was so DARK that I banged my snout against a column and gave myself a **black eye**!

"**YEE-OUCH!**" I shouted.

I tried to turn on the lights, but an **antique** chandelier fell right on top of me, **SCRAPING** my ear!

"**Owww!**" I howled.

As I hopped up and down in pain, a

floorboard popped up and **SLAMMED** down on my tail!

"***Ouch ouch ouchie!***"

Uncle Samuel strode in holding a candle stump. "Nephew, don't yell like that. You'll wear out your vocal cords!" he scolded me. "We can't spare the money to buy you **MEDICINE** for a sore throat!"

THIS ROOM FOR PAYING GUESTS ONLY!

Uncle Samuel's son, Stevie, followed him into the room. Stevie was a tall, thin rodent with a patched jacket. Behind him were Grandma and Grandpa Cheaperly, who were shaking their snouts at me sadly. "So you've turned into a big spender, eh, Geronimo?"

The Stingysnouts escorted me to my room. A strange SIGN hung on the door: THIS

ROOM FOR PAYING GUESTS ONLY!

I pushed open the squeaky door. In the candlelight, I saw an ancient, broken-down canopy bed.

I tried to close the curtain, which smelled of mold, but the canopy fell on my snout and left a **BIG BUMP**!

Next I tried to sit on a chair, but it had been chewed by **termites** and collapsed under me. When I tried to put it back together, I got a splinter in my **paw**!

Then I tried to lie down on the mattress, but there was a spring

sticking out, and it poked me in the tail! OOOOOWWWW!

As I was checking the BUMP on my snout, examining my wounded paw, and massaging my tail, Uncle Samuel approached me with his paw outstretched. "Okay, Nephew, time to pay up!"

I was astonished. "Wh-what? I thought I was your guest!"

"Didn't you see the sign on the door? This room is for paying guests only. You must pay for your stay. So paw over the dough! This is your first lesson, Nephew: If you want to save money, never give anything away for free!"

Why, that wasn't saving money, it was stinginess! But I wasn't in a position to protest.

"Uncle, you know very well that I don't

have any money," I replied.

Uncle Samuel sighed. "All right, because you're family, I'll let you barter. In return for the room, you can give me your nice **gold** watch."

Geronimo's watch, a gift from Thea

Dear reader, I really didn't want to paw over that watch. My sister, Thea, had given it to me years ago, and I loved it dearly. But I *had* to stay at **Moldy Manor** to complete my crash course and save *The Rodent's Gazette*!

Uncle Samuel snatched the watch out of my paws. Then he turned tail and left. "Good night, Nephew! Try not to DREAM too much — you need to save your energy!"

Once he was gone, I realized there were TEARS in my eyes. I was alone and desperate. I missed my cozy house; my super-comfy room; my super-full refrigerator; my little red fish, Hannibal; my family; and most of all, my darling nephew Benjamin.

I decided to call him, but I couldn't get a signal on my cell phone. Weird!

Instead, I thought I would take a HOT shower. I needed it after that ride in the manure cart!

I lathered up my fur and turned on the faucet. A jet of ice-cold water sprayed me in the snout. That's when I noticed another sign: INSERT COINS FOR HOT WATER. OTHERWISE, COLD WATER ONLY!

I didn't know what to do. Would I rather rinse off with cold water or have soapy fur?

I didn't want to catch a cold, so I decided to keep my fur sudsy. 1 But my boots were already filled with freezing water, and there was an icy draft blowing from a broken window. 2 So I caught a chill, anyway! 3 The sheets reeked of mold. I put a clothespin on my snout so I wouldn't

WHAT A NIGHT AT MOLDY MANOR!

suffocate from the stench. 4

The one thin blanket was infested with **fleas**. 5 Soon, I had bites all over . . . and my boots were still soaked with water, which made it impossible to sleep. 6

What an unbearable night at Moldy Manor!

5 FLEAS IN MY BLANKET BIT ME ALL OVER!

6 AND SLEEPING IN BOOTS SOAKED WITH WATER WAS DOWNRIGHT IMPOSSIBLE!

A Stingy Breakfast

The next morning, I got up early and headed down to the KITCHEN.

Uncle Samuel was there to greet me. "Nephew, eat some breakfast so you'll have energy for our crash course in saving."

My fur went WHITER than a mozzarella ball when I saw what was on the kitchen table. There was only:

1 DROP of milk in a thimble,

1 SLIVER of banana on a bottle cap (so we wouldn't have to wash a plate!),

1 PIECE of broken biscuit on 1 SQUARE of toilet paper (to save a napkin!).

"Geronimo, dear, don't forget you must pay for breakfast. Since you have no money, you can give me your vest instead."

Here's breakfast!
Where's the rest of it?

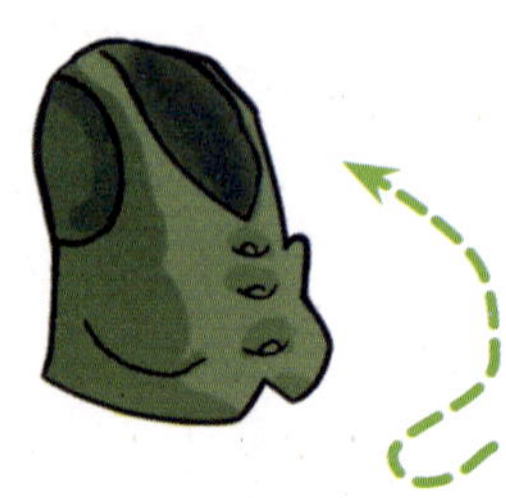

Geronimo's vest, a gift from Aunt Sweetfur

"But, Uncle . . ." I protested.

Uncle Samuel patted me on the tail. "If you want to eat, fork over the vest, Nephew!"

This time, I refused. My vest was a gift from Aunt Sweetfur, and I wasn't about to give it up for such a MINUSCULE meal. Even if I ate it, I'd still be starving!

Uncle Samuel didn't back down. "Very well, dear Nephew . . . today we will begin your personal crash course in saving. Your instructor is the greatest expert on saving money in the Valley of Thrift. He just happens to be my third cousin, twice removed — the very famouse Miserly Parsimouse. He's nicknamed the Wallet Watchrat because when it's time to PAY the bill, he automatically hides his wallet."

As Uncle Samuel was squeaking, the door **flung open**, and a rodent with gray fur strode in. He had on a **worn-out** gray jacket with a fake collar and cuffs sewn on (to save him from having to wear a **dress shirt**!).

Miserly's **shiny** gray pants were a **MASTERPIECE** of patchwork. He had a fake tie complete with a fake tiepin — it was stitched right on the collar of the shirt (also fake!). I

could tell that he **WASHED** himself with cold water instead of soap because he gave off the distinct **odor** of old cheese.

"I am **Miserly Parsimouse**, also called the Wallet Watchrat, and proud of it! I'm the greatest expert on saving money in the **Valley of Thrift**. I even wrote a book on the subject . . . Look!"

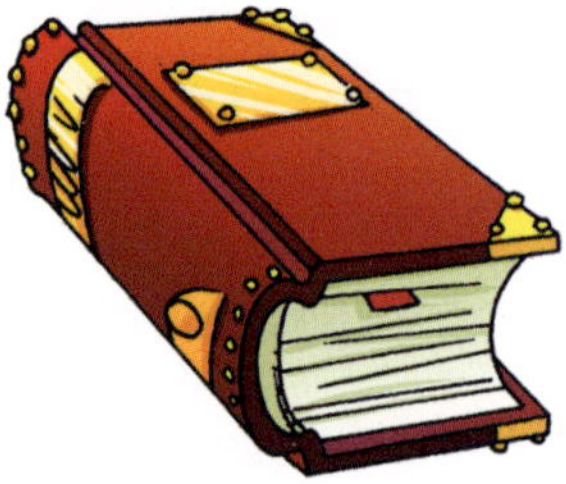

He placed a massive **BOOK** in my paws.

"To prepare for the crash course in saving, you must study my textbook, **Saving Money from A to Z**. I've patented this method! I was inspired by the teachings of my ancestor, Augustus 'Greedy Gus' Parsimouse. Now, there was a mouse who knew how to **save**. Compared to him, I am an amateur!"

Uncle Samuel was moved. "Learn from this mouse, Nephew! Take inspiration from him! Imitate him!" He dried a tear on my tie. "Can I use your tie as a tissue? I don't use tissues because I don't like to waste them!"

"Excuse me, Geronimo. My book is expensive." Miserly coughed. "But your uncle told me you don't have any money. If you want, I will accept your gold pen as payment . . ."

I took off my glasses so I could cry freely. I was so fond of that pen! But I gave it to Miserly. I had no choice!

Miserly pawed me the book. "And now study, study, study! You must learn this textbook by heart. Once you've mastered the theory, we will move on to its APPLICATION!"

Geronimo's gold pen, a gift from Grandfather William

And so I began reading the course description and **Miserly Parsimouse's** biography . . .

BECOME A SAVER IN THREE SIMPLE STINGY STEPS!

PUT THE PATENTED MISERLY METHOD INTO ACTION!

DAY ONE: EXPLORE MOLDY MANOR

TOUR THIS UNIQUE SUPER-SAVER HOUSE, DESIGNED BY AUTHOR MISERLY PARSIMOUSE.

DAY TWO: VISIT THRIFTY CITY

LEARN ALL THE BEST TRICKS FOR WATCHING YOUR WALLET WHILE YOU SHOP.

DAY THREE: THE MISERMOUSE FINAL EXAM

MISERLY PARSIMOUSE, nicknamed the WALLET WATCHRAT for his stinginess, is the biggest expert on saving money in the VALLEY OF THRIFT. He graduated from Cheaprat College at the top of his class, majoring in stinginess and saving. Parsimouse's manual *SAVING MONEY FROM A TO Z* became an instant bestseller.

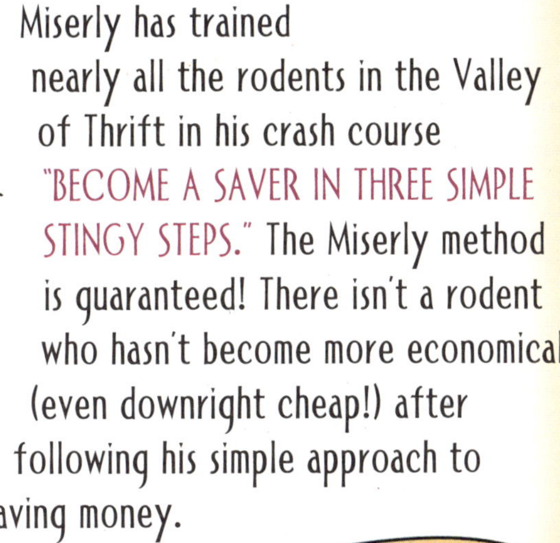

Miserly has trained nearly all the rodents in the Valley of Thrift in his crash course "BECOME A SAVER IN THREE SIMPLE STINGY STEPS." The Miserly method is guaranteed! There isn't a rodent who hasn't become more economical (even downright cheap!) after following his simple approach to saving money.

Day One: A Thrifty House

My **CRASH COURSE** began at ten a.m. sharp.

Miserly called me into **Moldy Manor's** grimy study, where no one ever dusted — Uncle Samuel didn't want to waste the feathers in the feather duster!

"Okay, **big spender**, over the next three days, I'll take your extravagant ideas on spending and transform them into ways to save! Stick with me, and you'll become a **THRIFTY MOUSE**. You have the word of Miserly Parsimouse, the Number One Saver in **Thrifty City**!"

I was a little glum about getting a personalized crash course from Miserly.

Was I so HOPELESS that I needed help from Mouse Island's GREATEST expert? Sighing, I began to take notes.

"Our first lesson will be how to run a thrifty house," Miserly squeaked. "Tomorrow, you'll visit Thrifty City so that you can learn to resist the temptation to shop. On our third and final day, you'll take my final EXAM."

I knew these next three days would be unbearable. But I had to make Grandfather happy. And I absolutely had to hold on to *The Rodent's Gazette*! So I just nodded and held my tongue.

Miserly pulled out a crumpled old cheese wrapper and wrote

Geronimo's Report Card across the top. "I will give you a plus for each question you answer correctly, and a MINUS for each one you answer incorrectly!" he said solemnly.

Miserly began listing his favorite tricks for saving money. "Let's start with the kitchen. First, put a padlock on your pantry. That way, you won't be able to eat too much, and you'll save a bundle on food. Also, the less you clean, the better off you are. You'll save on rags, and you won't SCRATCH the furniture. Plus, you won't exert yourself, so you won't need to eat as much, which will save money on food! And you won't sweat, so you won't waste WATER washing yourself, and you won't need to change your clothes!"

Miserly grinned at me. "The ideal would be

to learn to not breathe, so you don't waste **air**, but no one has ever figured out a way to do that. My great-great-great-grandfather tried, but he **DIED** during the course of the experiment, poor rodent!"

We went into the living room, where the **furniture** was still covered with plastic like it had been the day it was delivered.

Miserly pointed at the chairs and couches proudly. “See? Your uncle never unwrapped them, so they won’t be **damaged**! What a brilliant way to save!”

In the fireplace, there were **FLAMES**,

but it was so cold in the room, I realized they were painted on.

"Are the flames painted on to **save** wood?" I asked Miserly.

Miserly marked a plus on my **REPORT CARD**. "Very good! See, you're already beginning to catch on."

We **headed** for the bathroom. "Remember:

Don't use energy and you won't **sweat**, and then you won't have to wash yourself," Miserly advised me.

Then it was time for the **bedroom**. Miserly kept me there for hours, explaining all the secrets to saving.

We finished the lesson in the hallway, where he showed me the **wallpaper**. It was

made of paper scraps glued to the wall . . . **to save** money, obviously!

At the end of the day, Miserly said good-bye. "Sleep well, Geronimo! Tomorrow we'll be ***busy*** with your tour of Thrifty City."

Despite all the energy I'd saved, I was exhausted!

I was also starving. I ran to the **Kitchen**, where Uncle Samuel was waiting for me. "Ah, Nephew, you're **TOO LATE**! Dinner has already been served, and there's nothing left over. I'm sorry, but you simply must get here earlier."

"But I was at my lesson!" I protested.

"Okay, I'll prepare my **specialty** for you: The very tasty **Stingysnout Special** . . . in exchange for your nice

Geronimo's belt, a gift from Trap

red **BELT**!"

This time, I **COULDN'T** refuse. I was hungrier than a rodent on a MouseFast diet. I chomped on a **teeny-tiny** sandwich: two slices of stale bread with a crust of cheese and a **drop** of rancid mayonnaise, topped with a sliver of **MOLDY** cucumber.

"By the way, did you squeak to Benjamin?" Uncle Samuel asked. "He phoned earlier and said he wanted to squeak to you, but he didn't say **WHY**."

The thought of Benjamin cheered me up. "**Oh, great!** I'll call him back now."

Uncle Samuel **POINTED** at the ancient phone hanging on the wall. "Oh, sorry, this **TELEPHONE** only receives

Geronimo's cell phone

calls — you **CAN'T** call out from here. And don't bother trying to use your cell phone. There's no service!"

I let out a deep sigh. Well, at least I'd save money on my phone bill!

There was nothing left to do but go to bed. At least I didn't have to take another **cold shower** — with all the energy I'd saved, there was no need to wash up!

Day Two: Thrifty City

At breakfast the next day, I was ravenous. For a fee, **Uncle Samuel** prepared me a slice of toast **spread** with a light layer of cream cheese. I devoured it. After I finished, I even picked up all the crumbs off the table and ate them!

Geronimo's jacket, a present from Aunt Sugarfur

Uncle Samuel approved. "Well done, Nephew. See, you've already learned not to waste A SINGLE CRUMB!"

In exchange for the toast, he made me give him my jacket.

That day was reserved for a tour of Thrifty City, the capital of the Valley of Thrift. Miserly came to get me — on paw, naturally, so as not to waste gasoline. I would have preferred not to walk, since the green boots were pinching my toes more than ever, but I didn't want to waste any energy protesting!

When we arrived in Spendthrift Square, the center of Thrifty City, I looked around curiously. The signs on all the stores were shut off.

"What time do the stores open here?" I asked Miserly.

Miserly shook his snout. "What a waste of a breath that question is, Stilton! The stores are already open, but the signs are obviously turned off to save money!" He marked a MINUS on my report card.

I smacked myself on the snout. What a cheesebrain I was! I should have known why the signs were all off: to save electricity, of course!

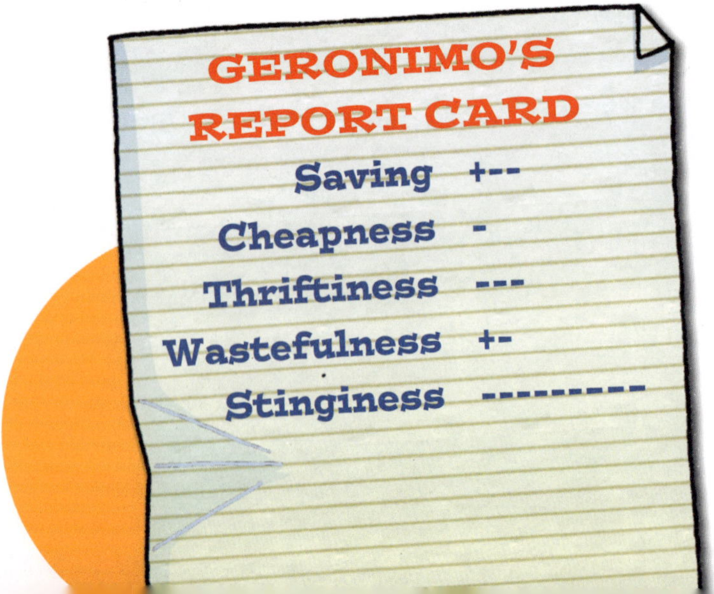

GERONIMO'S REPORT CARD

Saving +--

Cheapness -

Thriftiness ---

Wastefulness +-

Stinginess ---------

I **SPOTTED** a rodent pushing a motorcycle with the engine turned off. Thinking it was **broken**, I went over to help him.

The rodent was offended. "Mister, has the cheese slipped off your cracker? There's nothing wrong with my motorcycle. I'm just pushing it to **save** gas, naturally!"

Miserly marked another **MINUS** on my report card. But this time, he didn't bother saying a thing — to save his breath!

What a sillysnout I was! I was trying my hardest, but I couldn't be as stingy as Miserly and Uncle Samuel. It just wasn't in me!

I began to get very thirsty. That toast spread with cream cheese was going up and down in my stomach like a roller coaster at Mouseyworld. I needed to drink something, but I knew better than to ask Miserly to buy WATER. I didn't want any more MINUSES on my report card!

I looked around for a water fountain, but there wasn't ONE. That's when I saw a bicycle with IRON wheels pass by.

Miserly sighed. Predicting my question, he said, "The wheels are made of iron to avoid wearing out the rubber tires, naturally!"

By now, I was **parched**. When I saw a fountain, I dashed over to get a drink, but . . . surprise! In Thrifty City, even the public water FOUNTAINS have a fee.

"How much does it cost?" I asked Miserly.

"Too much! Wait till we're back at Moldy Manor, Geronimo," he replied.

I was **terribly thirsty**, but Miserly led me away by the paw, saying, "Enough wasting time! Now we'll begin a new lesson on how to resist the temptation of shopping. After today, you won't be a **BIG SPENDER** anymore. You have the Miserly guarantee!"

As we scampered along Main Street, I spotted many signs for **sales**. To help me resist the temptation, Miserly put a **MOUSETRAP** in my wallet. He made me wear special mittens with a **padlock** on the wrists so I wouldn't be able to sign any checks.

Then he gave me a **MousePod** with headphones. I was hoping for some relaxing music, but it turned out to be Miserly's squeak repeating the words, "Friends don't let friends spend!"

Finally, he made me put on dark **glasses** so I wouldn't be lured into shops. Unfortunately, the glasses were so dark I couldn't see a thing . . . and scampered straight into a lamppost!

Ouchie! That hurt!

Day Three: The Misermouse Final Exam

At the end of the day, I was zonked. But that NIGHT, I never closed my eyes. Between the fleas biting my fur and the boots pinching my paws, I was in AGONY!

The next morning, my eyelids were heavier than a pound of petrified Parmesan. I could hardly move. But I reminded myself it was the *last* day. I could take the test, and then I could GO HOME.

I dragged my sorry tail into the living room of Moldy Manor. Miserly was there waiting for me. Solemnly, he pawed me the Misermouse FINAL EXAM. "I recommend you answer these questions

honestly, Geronimo!" he advised me.

I sat at the desk and began to read the **TEST**. Holey cheese, if I answered honestly, I'd **NEVER** pass it! I swear on a block of cheddar, I am not now, nor will I ever be, a penny-pincher!

I couldn't bring myself to **lie**. I just couldn't fake it!

When I'd finished, I pawed my **PAPER** back to Miserly. "I'm sorry, but I don't think I passed the test." I sighed. "I can't pretend to be stingy. I like to share what I have with

THE MISERMOUSE FINAL EXAM

1. IT'S THE BIRTHDAY OF YOUR SECOND COUSIN, ONCE REMOVED. YOU . . .

A. Buy her very expensive cheesy chocolates.
B. Send a box of chocolates you've already opened, but you wrap it nicely.
C. Send an affectionate birthday card.
D. Pretend you forgot, just like last year.

2. WHEN YOU'RE HEADING TO WORK, YOU . . .

A. Drive yourself. Gas is expensive, but driving is comfortable and easy.
B. Take the subway.
C. Walk. That's the healthy way.
D. Make your friend come pick you up — it's cheaper that way.

3. HOW OFTEN DO YOU BORROW YOUR NEIGHBOR'S BICYCLE?

A. Never
B. Occasionally
C. About once a week
D. So often that my neighbor has to borrow it back from me!

4. YOU NEED TO MAKE A PHONE CALL. YOU . . .

A. Grab your cell phone and start dialing.
B. Wait till you're home, then call from a landline.
C. Make the call short, using as few minutes as possible.
D. Stop someone on the street and ask to borrow his phone, saying it's an emergency!

5. WHEN YOU'RE ON VACATION, YOU . . .

A. Don't care what you spend.
B. Choose the place that has the best quality for the best price.
C. Spend as little money as possible on transportation and hotel.
D. Tag along on a friend's vacation. Isn't that what friends are for?

6. YOU ARE INVITED TO A BLACK-TIE PARTY. YOU . . .

A. Buy a very expensive designer tuxedo.
B. Rent a nice-looking tuxedo.
C. Borrow a tuxedo from your cousin who's a foot shorter than you. It's better than nothing, and it's free!
D. Have a new tuxedo hanging in your closet, but you go in sweatpants. You don't want to ruin your new tux!

7. YOU WANT TO IMPRESS A RODENT YOU'VE JUST MET. YOU . . .

A. Send her two dozen red roses.
B. Bring her a bouquet of flowers you bought at the supermarket.
C. Visit the cemetery — there are always free flowers there!
D. Invite her out to dinner and make her pay!

ANSWER KEY: A TRUE MISERMOUSE ALWAYS PICKS D!

my friends, and now that I have less, it just means that I will have less to share.

"Miserly, I want to thank you," I continued. "Your CRASH COURSE really taught me how to save money, even if it's more of a course on stinginess than on saving!"

Miserly's snout was filled with emotion. He dried a tear and wiped his snout on my tie (to avoid wasting TISSUES, of course).

"SNIFF . . . that was beautiful, Geronimo! I am moved," he said. "Although we are very different, and you are a shameless SQUANDERER, I've come to respect you."

I shook his paw. "I respect

you, too. Thank you for everything you've taught me."

Miserly squeezed my **paw**. "How wonderful! Now we're the best of friends! But you still need to **PAY** for the crash course. I never give credit, especially not to my friends."

"Um, I would like to pay you, but I really don't know how I can . . . " I said.

He raised an eyebrow and pointed to my **boots**. "What about those?"

I shrugged. "It's a deal. If you can get them off, **they're all yours**!"

Miserly soon realized he'd

gotten more than he'd bargained for. He called in the whole Stingysnout family to help. Together, they began to **PULL . . . AND PULL . . . AND PULL . . .** Suddenly, there was a loud pop, and my paws were free at last!

Thank goodmouse! What a relief! And pee-yoo, what stinky paws!

It was time to say good-bye. I really wanted to know the results of the **test**, but Miserly said he'd promised to tell Grandfather first.

I **scurried** home to my snug little

mousehole. I was **weary**, worn, **wiped out** . . . and absolutely starving!

In the fridge, I had nothing but **LEFTOVER** cheese rinds. They seemed a little hard, but I ate them anyway. They couldn't be worse than the meals at **Moldy Manor**.

How delicious they tasted!

How **soft** my bed felt!

And how cozy my apartment was!

But despite all the comforts of home, I was still stressed about my score on the test.

Bad News . . . and Good News!

The next morning, my doorbell rang early. It was Benjamin and Grandfather Shortpaws! I was thrilled to see them.

"Grandson, how was the **CRASH COURSE IN SAVING**?" Grandfather demanded.

"It wasn't a crash course in saving; it was an advanced course in **stinginess**!" I replied. "It was **terrible**. I only stayed because my bank account is at **ZERO** and I didn't want to lose *The Rodent's Gazette*. So, tell me, how did I do on the test?"

My whiskers trembled with anxiety as I waited for Grandfather's answer.

"Er, well, Grandson, I have bad news and good news," Grandfather said.

I had a feeling my grandfather was nervous. **BUT WHY?** Grandfather never got nervous about anything!

"Look, Geronimo, let me — what I need to tell you is . . . " he stammered. Then he took a deep breath. "The **bad news** is you **didn't** pass the test."

I tore at my fur. "Oh no! I've lost *The Rodent's Gazette*!" I cried.

Grandfather cut me off before I could squeak another word. "But the good news is that you have **MORE THAN ZERO** dollars in your bank account!"

"What?!" I shrieked. "But I saw the balance with my own two eyes! My account was down to **ZERO**!"

Grandfather snorted. "Geronimo, your account showed a balance of **ZERO** on Sunday morning. But on Monday your bank called to say there was an **ERROR**. You actually still had money in your account!"

I **sighed** with relief. "So everything is okay! Why didn't you tell me right away?"

"I called you, but you didn't answer the phone, and at **Moldy Manor**, you can't call back," Benjamin squeaked.

"Well, Grandson, I hope you're not going to complain," Grandfather said. "The ***CRASH COURSE*** was good for you. In the future, you should think twice before you spend!"

It was true: The course had been **GOOD** for me. I would never become stingy, but the class had helped me understand the importance of saving — so that I'd have more to ***share*** with others!

Just then the telephone rang.

RIIIING, RIIIIIIING, RIIIIIIIING!

"Hello, this is Geronimo Stilton!" I said, picking it up.

It was my dear friend Nutty Chocorat. "Hi, Geronimo!" he cried enthusiastically.

It was a smash success!

"While you were away, I opened OUR store, Chocorat's Choc-o-Rama. It's been a smash success! Our cheesy chocolates have SOLD OUT, and we've MADE A FORTUNE!"

How fabumouse! I passed on the news, and my grandfather congratulated me.

"Grandson, I must admit you were right to make that investment," he said grumpily. "I knew the store would do well. In business, you must take risks to succeed. You took a risk, and it paid off. WELL DONE!"

To celebrate, I invited the whole family and all my friends to Nutty's new chocolate SHOP. I even asked Trap along, although he was the one who made this mess and then left me alone to flail like a fly in fondue! But

I can never stay **MAD** at my cousin for long.

I also invited all the Stingysnouts, who eagerly accepted (only because it was free, of course!).

Nutty had dozens of **chocolates** to sample, and everyone crowded around to try them. **Yum!**

And so this strange adventure ends as happily as it began. I thought I'd **LOST** everything, but instead I learned a lot and made a new friend. I discovered the art of **saving**, but also the importance of staying true to myself.

See you next time, dear reader! Till then, I'll be surrounded by my **loved ones**, chewing on the finest chocolates on Mouse Island!

Be sure to read all my fabumouse adventures!

#1 Lost Treasure of the Emerald Eye

#2 The Curse of the Cheese Pyramid

#3 Cat and Mouse in a Haunted House

#4 I'm Too Fond of My Fur!

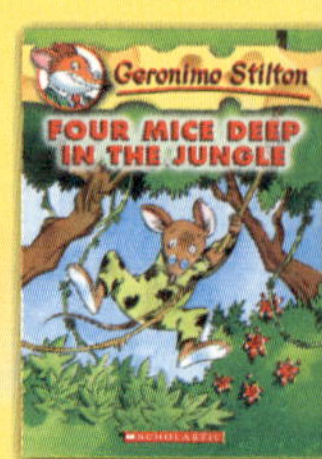

#5 Four Mice Deep in the Jungle

#6 Paws Off, Cheddarface!

#7 Red Pizzas for a Blue Count

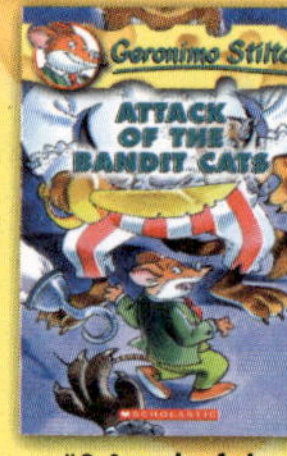

#8 Attack of the Bandit Cats

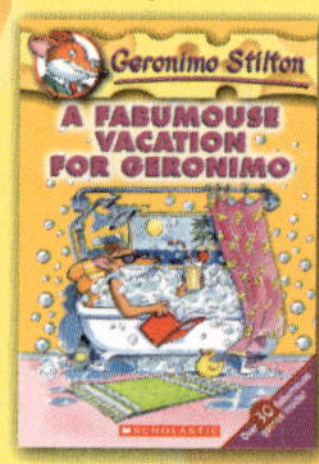

#9 A Fabumouse Vacation for Geronimo

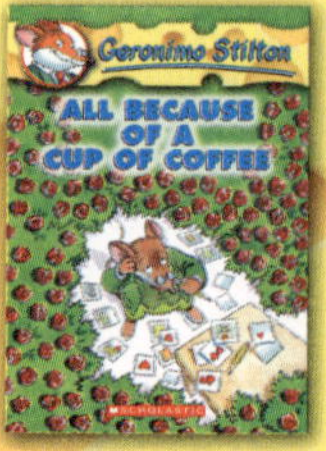

#10 All Because of a Cup of Coffee

#11 It's Halloween, You 'Fraidy Mouse!

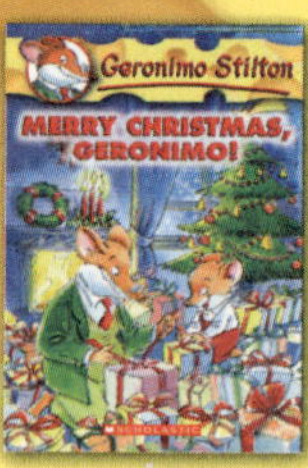

#12 Merry Christmas, Geronimo!

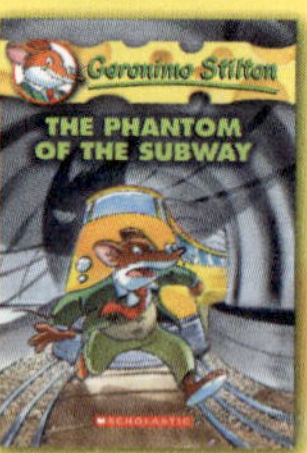

#13 The Phantom of the Subway

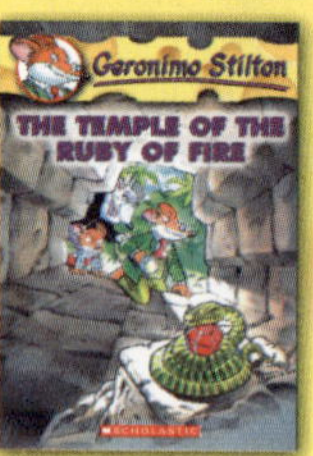

#14 The Temple of the Ruby of Fire

#15 The Mona Mousa Code

#16 A Cheese-Colored Camper

#17 Watch Your Whiskers, Stilton!

#18 Shipwreck on the Pirate Islands

#19 My Name Is Stilton, Geronimo Stilton

#20 Surf's Up, Geronimo!

#21 The Wild, Wild West

#22 The Secret of Cacklefur Castle

A Christmas Tale

#23 Valentine's Day Disaster

#24 Field Trip to Niagara Falls

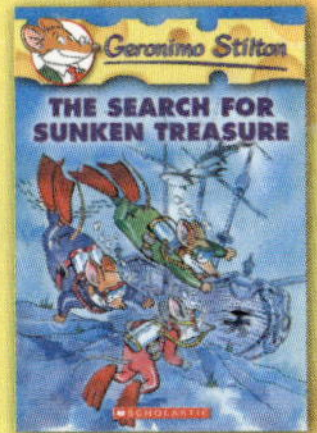

#25 The Search for Sunken Treasure

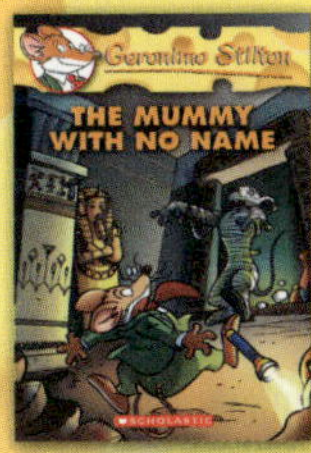

#26 The Mummy with No Name

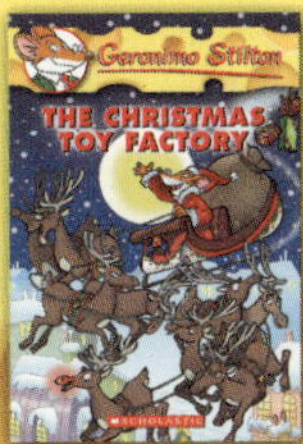

#27 The Christmas Toy Factory

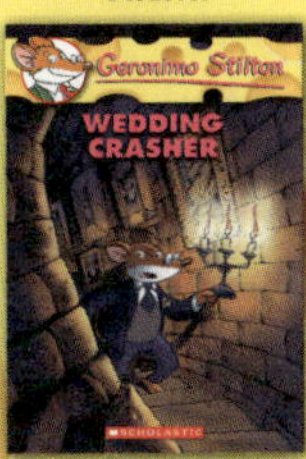

#28 Wedding Crasher

#29 Down and Out Down Under

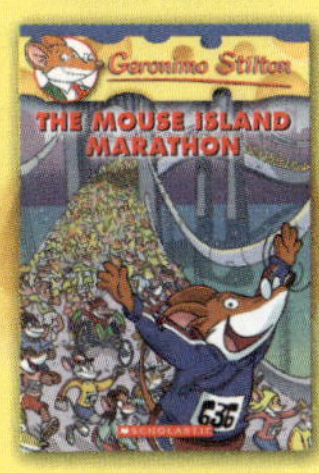

#30 The Mouse Island Marathon

#31 The Mysterious Cheese Thief

Christmas Catastrophe

#32 Valley of the Giant Skeletons

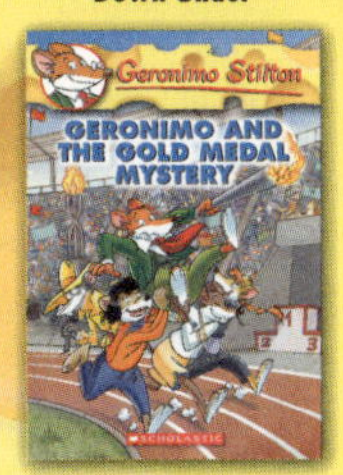

#33 Geronimo and the Gold Medal Mystery

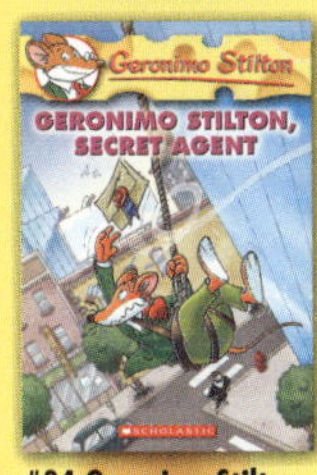

#34 Geronimo Stilton, Secret Agent

#35 A Very Merry Christmas

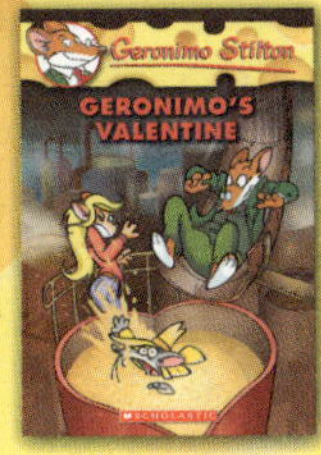

#36 Geronimo's Valentine

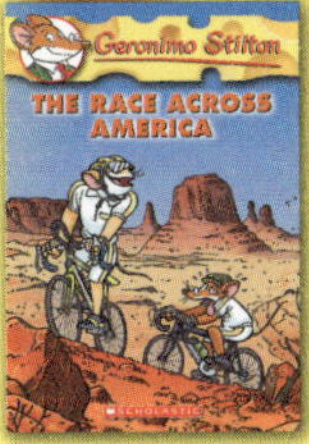

#37 The Race Across America

#38 A Fabumouse School Adventure

#39 Singing Sensation

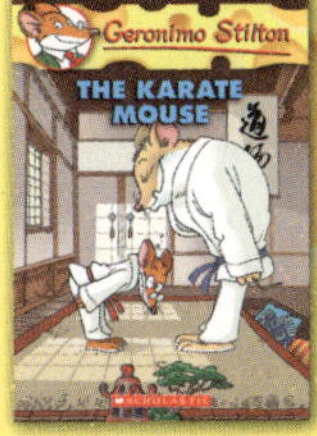

#40 The Karate Mouse

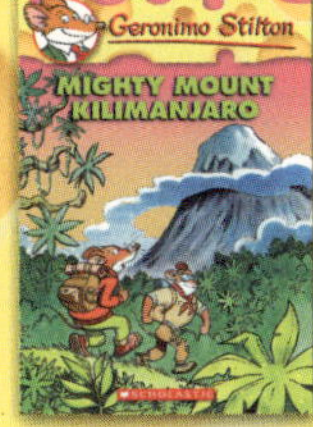

#41 Mighty Mount Kilimanjaro

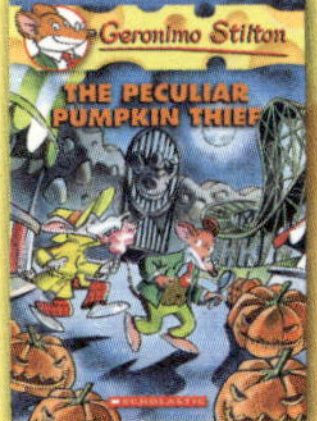

#42 The Peculiar Pumpkin Thief

#43 I'm Not a Supermouse!

#44 The Giant Diamond Robbery

#45 Save the White Whale!

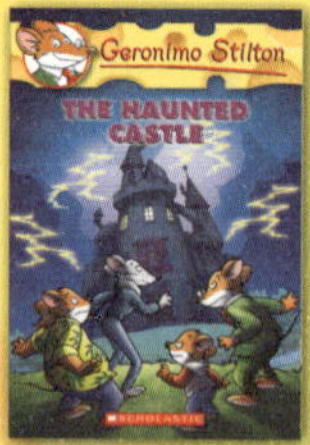

#46 The Haunted Castle

#47 Run for the Hills, Geronimo!

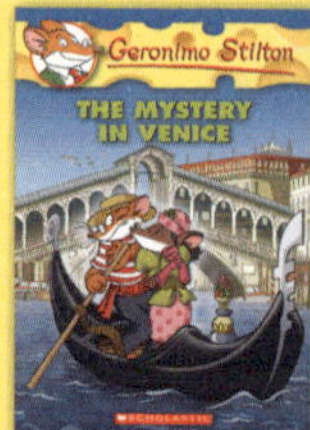

#48 The Mystery in Venice

#49 The Way of the Samurai

#50 This Hotel Is Haunted!

#51 The Enormouse Pearl Heist

#52 Mouse in Space!

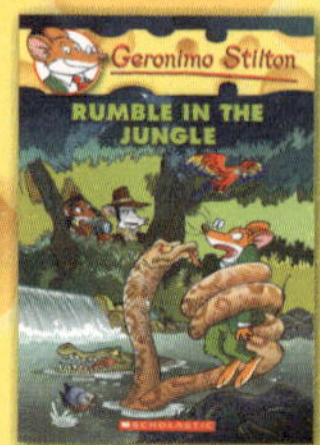

#53 Rumble in the Jungle

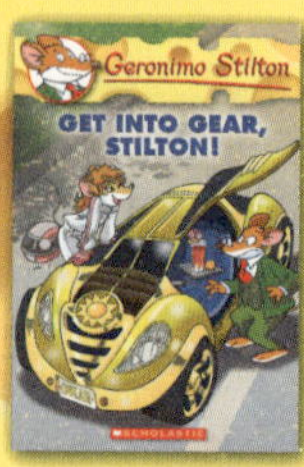

#54 Get into Gear, Stilton!

#55 The Golden Statue Plot

#56 Flight of the Red Bandit

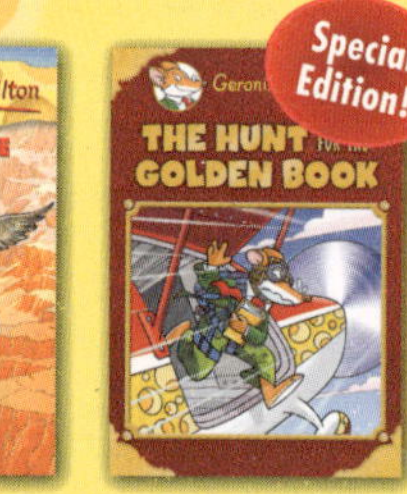

The Hunt for the Golden Book

#57 The Stinky Cheese Vacation

#58 The Super Chef Contest

#59 Welcome to Moldy Manor

The Hunt for the Curious Cheese

#60 The Treasure of Easter Island

Join me and my friends as we journey through time in these very special editions!

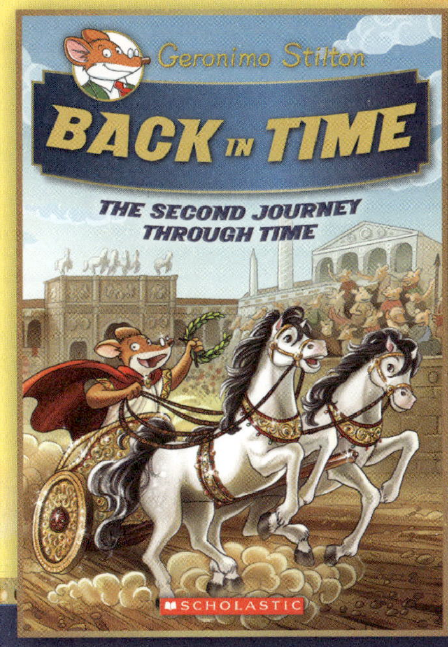

THE JOURNEY THROUGH TIME

BACK IN TIME:
THE SECOND JOURNEY THROUGH TIME

Don't miss these exciting Thea Sisters adventures!

Thea Stilton and the Dragon's Code

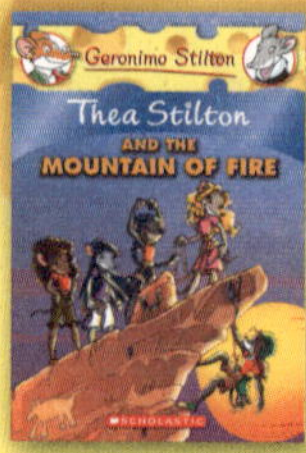

Thea Stilton and the Mountain of Fire

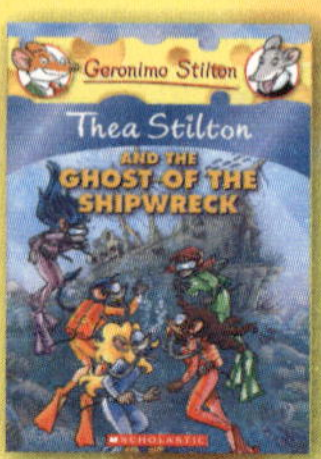

Thea Stilton and the Ghost of the Shipwreck

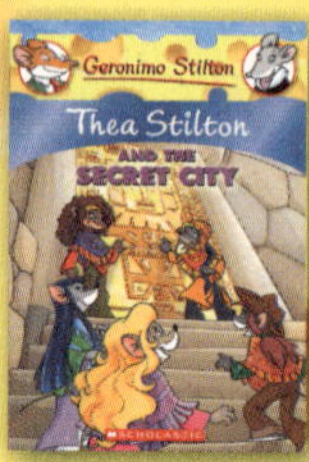

Thea Stilton and the Secret City

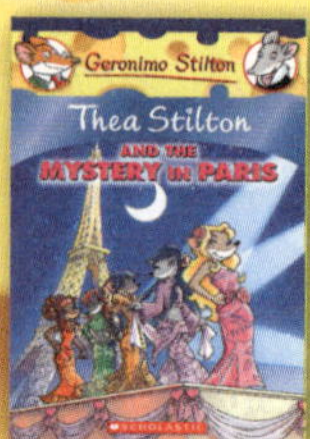

Thea Stilton and the Mystery in Paris

Thea Stilton and the Cherry Blossom Adventure

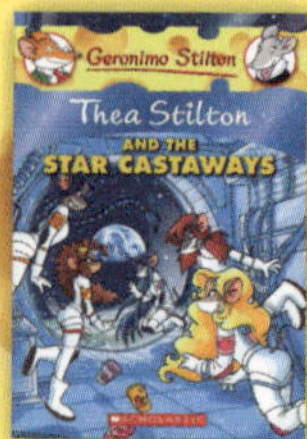

Thea Stilton and the Star Castaways

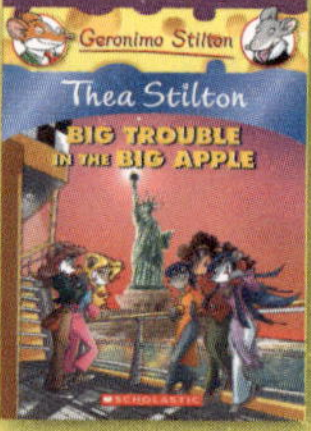

Thea Stilton: Big Trouble in the Big Apple

Thea Stilton and the Ice Treasure

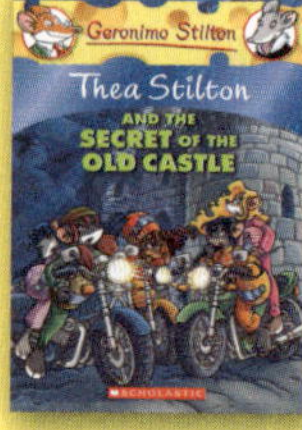

Thea Stilton and the Secret of the Old Castle

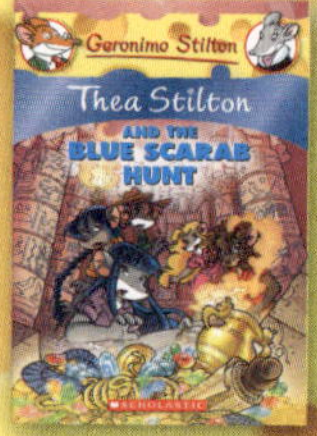

Thea Stilton and the Blue Scarab Hunt

Thea Stilton and the Prince's Emerald

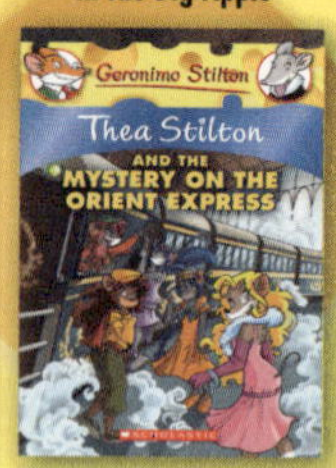

Thea Stilton and the Mystery on the Orient Express

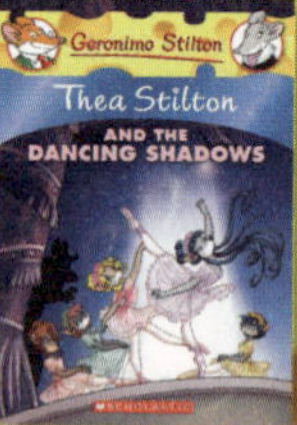

Thea Stilton and the Dancing Shadows

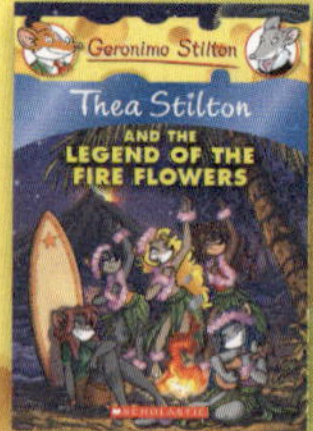

Thea Stilton and the Legend of the Fire Flowers

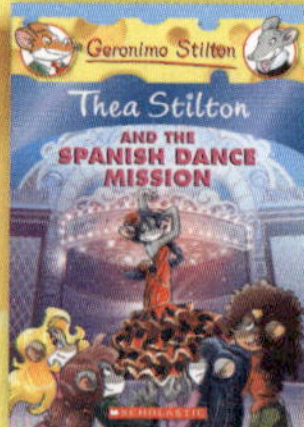

Thea Stilton and the Spanish Dance Mission

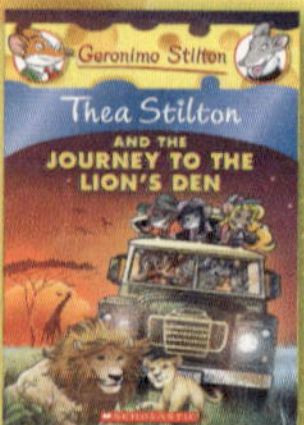

Thea Stilton and the Journey to the Lion's Den

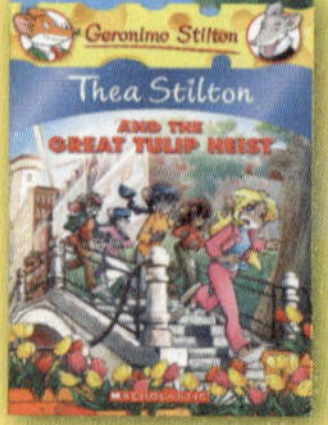

Thea Stilton and the Great Tulip Heist

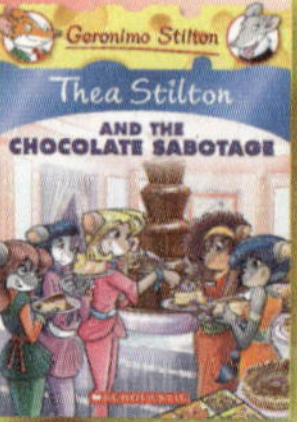

Thea Stilton and the Chocolate Sabotage

Thea Stilton and the Missing Myth

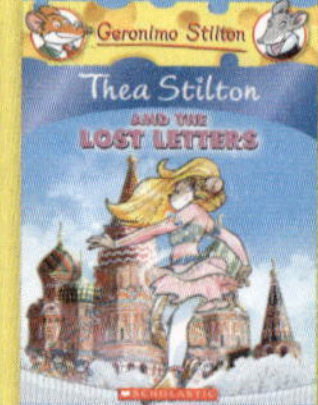

Thea Stilton and the Lost Letters

Be sure to read all of our magical special edition adventures!

The Kingdom of Fantasy

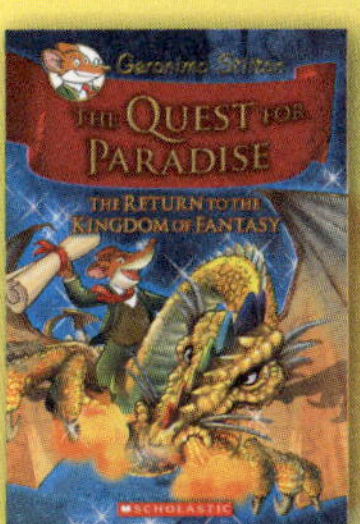

The Quest for Paradise:
The Return to the Kingdom of Fantasy

The Amazing Voyage:
The Third Adventure in the Kingdom of Fantasy

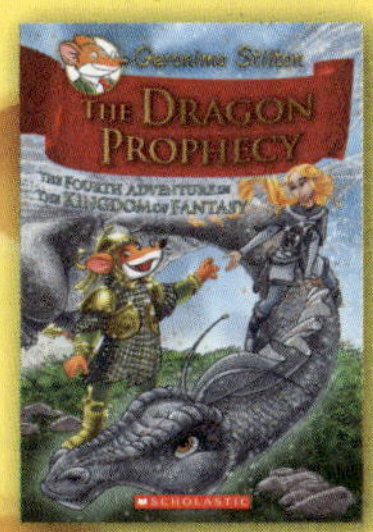

The Dragon Prophecy:
The Fourth Adventure in the Kingdom of Fantasy

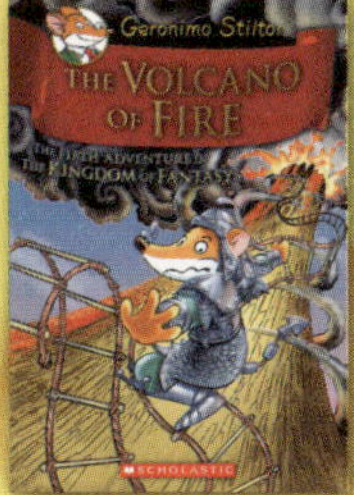

The Volcano of Fire:
The Fifth Adventure in the Kingdom of Fantasy

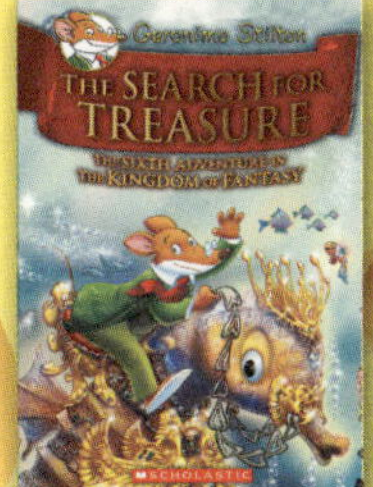

The Search for Treasure:
The Sixth Adventure in the Kingdom of Fantasy

The Enchanted Charms:
The Seventh Adventure in the Kingdom of Fantasy

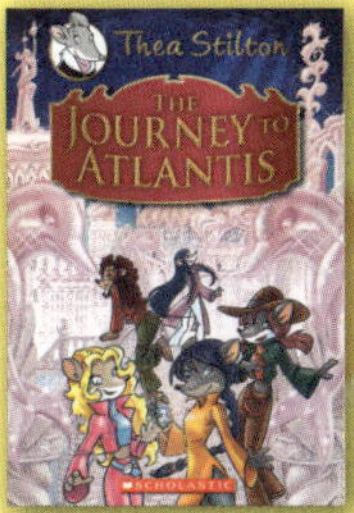

Thea Stilton: The Journey to Atlantis

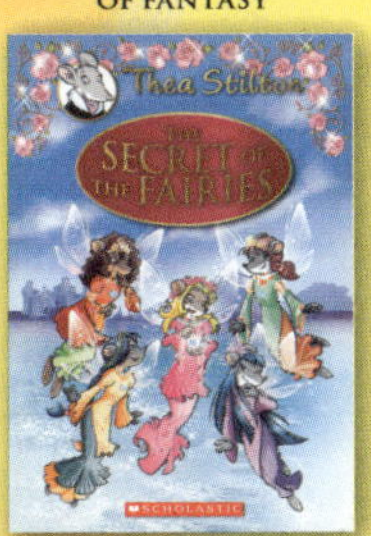

Thea Stilton: The Secret of the Fairies

Thea Stilton: The Secret of the Snow

MEET GERONIMO STILTONIX

He is a spacemouse — the Geronimo Stilton of a parallel universe! He is captain of the spaceship *MouseStar 1*. While flying through the cosmos, he visits distant planets and meets crazy aliens. His adventures are out of this world!

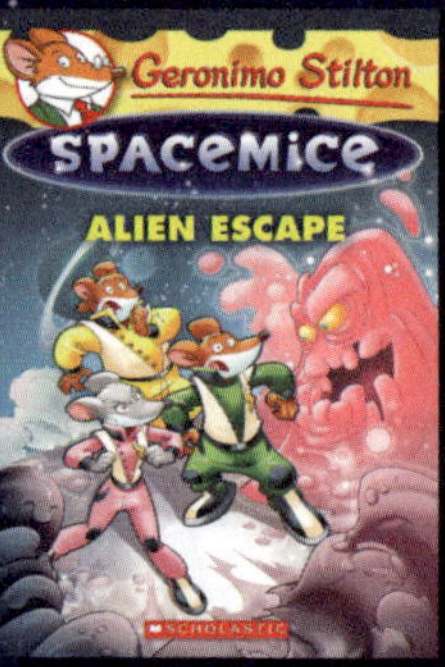

#1 Alien Escape

#2 You're Mine, Captain!

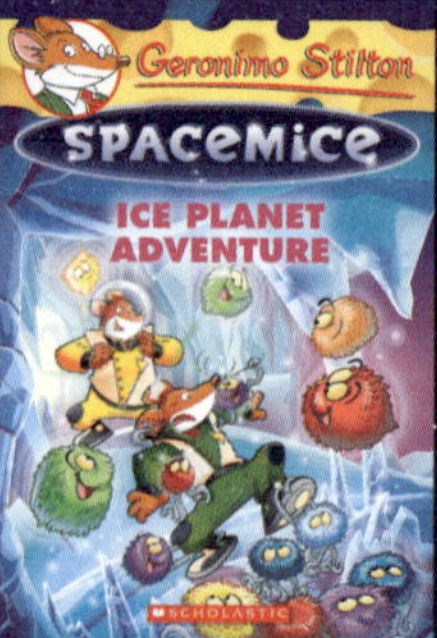

#3 Ice Planet Adventure

#4 The Galactic Goal

Meet GERONIMO STILTONOOT

He is a cavemouse — Geronimo Stilton's ancient ancestor! He runs the stone newspaper in the prehistoric village of Old Mouse City. From dealing with dinosaurs to dodging meteorites, his life in the Stone Age is full of adventure!

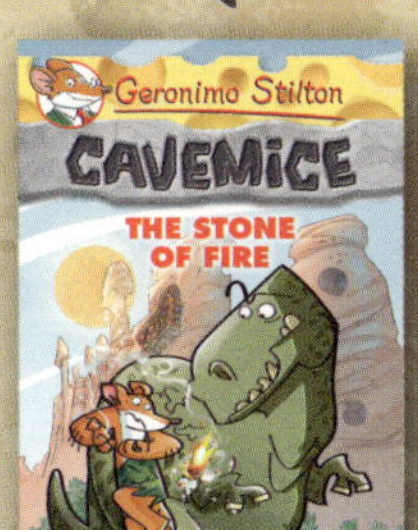

#1 The Stone of Fire

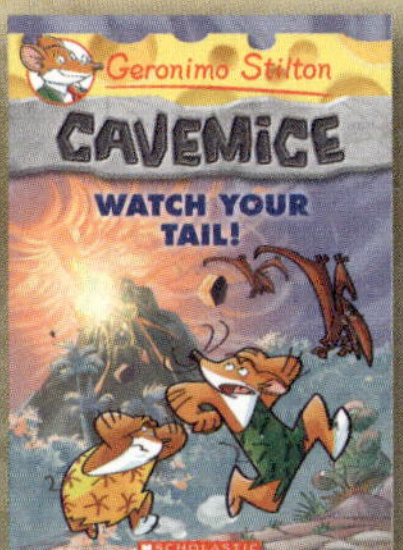

#2 Watch Your Tail!

#3 Help, I'm in Hot Lava!

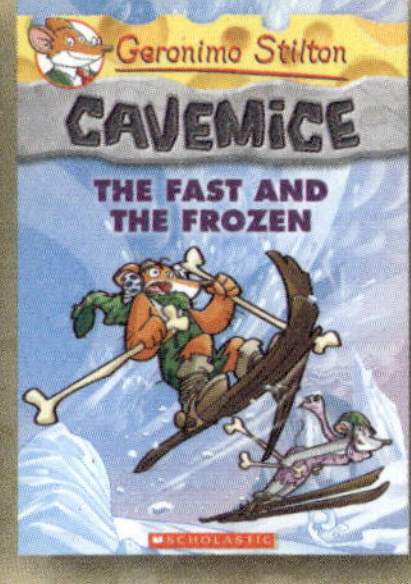

#4 The Fast and the Frozen

#5 The Great Mouse Race

#6 Don't Wake the Dinosaur!

#7 I'm a Scaredy-Mouse!

#8 Surfing for Secrets

About the Author

Born in New Mouse City, Mouse Island, **Geronimo Stilton** is Rattus Emeritus of Mousomorphic Literature and of Neo-Ratonic Comparative Philosophy. For the past twenty years, he has been running *The Rodent's Gazette*, New Mouse City's most widely read daily newspaper.

Stilton was awarded the Ratitzer Prize for his scoops on *The Curse of the Cheese Pyramid* and *The Search for Sunken Treasure*. He has also received the Andersen 2000 Prize for Personality of the Year. One of his bestsellers won the 2002 eBook Award for world's best ratlings' electronic book. His works have been published all over the globe.

In his spare time, Mr. Stilton collects antique cheese rinds and plays golf. But what he most enjoys is telling stories to his nephew Benjamin.

6
5
4
3
2
1
1. Main entrance
2. Printing presses (where the books and newspaper are printed)
3. Accounts department
4. Editorial room (where the editors, illustrators, and designers work)
5. Geronimo Stilton's office
6. Helicopter landing pad
THE RODENT'S GAZETTE

1
2
3
4
5
6
7
8
9
10
11
12
13
14
15
16
17
18
19
20
21
22
23
24
25
26
27
28
29
30
31
32
33
34
35
36
37
38
39
40
41
42
43
44
45
46
RODENT
RIVER
Beach

Map of New Mouse City

1. Industrial Zone
2. Cheese Factories
3. Angorat International Airport
4. WRAT Radio and Television Station
5. Cheese Market
6. Fish Market
7. Town Hall
8. Snotnose Castle
9. The Seven Hills of Mouse Island
10. Mouse Central Station
11. Trade Center
12. Movie Theater
13. Gym
14. Catnegie Hall
15. Singing Stone Plaza
16. The Gouda Theater
17. Grand Hotel
18. Mouse General Hospital
19. Botanical Gardens
20. Cheap Junk for Less (Trap's store)
21. Aunt Sweetfur and Benjamin's House
22. Mouseum of Modern Art
23. University and Library
24. *The Daily Rat*
25. *The Rodent's Gazette*
26. Trap's House
27. Fashion District
28. The Mouse House Restaurant
29. Environmental Protection Center
30. Harbor Office
31. Mousidon Square Garden
32. Golf Course
33. Swimming Pool
34. Tennis Courts
35. Curlyfur Island Amousement Park
36. Geronimo's House
37. Historic District
38. Public Library
39. Shipyard
40. Thea's House
41. New Mouse Harbor
42. Luna Lighthouse
43. The Statue of Liberty
44. Hercule Poirat's Office
45. Petunia Pretty Paws's House
46. Grandfather William's House

This way to the Rodent Straits
Brigand's Isle
Pirate Ship of Cats
Tomcat Island
Cat's Claw Bay
Panther Archipelago
Hamster Islands
Blue Dolphin Bay
Coral Reefs
This way to the Mousific Ocean
Swissvi
Cheddarton
Stray Cat Harbor
Mouseport
San Mouscisco
This way to the Ratlantic Ocean
New Mouse City
Mousefort Beach
N
W
E
S
Furflung Island
MOUSE ISLAND
This way to the Sea of Mice
1
2
3
4
5
6
7
8
9
10
11
12
13
14
15
16
17
18
19
20
21
22
23
24
25
26
27
28
29
30
31
32
33
34
35
36
37

Map of Mouse Island

1. Big Ice Lake
2. Frozen Fur Peak
3. Slipperyslopes Glacier
4. Coldcreeps Peak
5. Ratzikistan
6. Transratania
7. Mount Vamp
8. Roastedrat Volcano
9. Brimstone Lake
10. Poopedcat Pass
11. Stinko Peak
12. Dark Forest
13. Vain Vampires Valley
14. Goose Bumps Gorge
15. The Shadow Line Pass
16. Penny Pincher Castle
17. Nature Reserve Park
18. Las Ratayas Marinas
19. Fossil Forest
20. Lake Lake
21. Lake Lakelake
22. Lake Lakelakelake
23. Cheddar Crag
24. Cannycat Castle
25. Valley of the Giant Sequoia
26. Cheddar Springs
27. Sulfurous Swamp
28. Old Reliable Geyser
29. Vole Vale
30. Ravingrat Ravine
31. Gnat Marshes
32. Munster Highlands
33. Mousehara Desert
34. Oasis of the Sweaty Camel
35. Cabbagehead Hill
36. Rattytrap Jungle
37. Rio Mosquito

Dear mouse friends,
Thanks for reading, and farewell
till the next book.
It'll be another whisker-licking-good
adventure, and that's a promise!

Geronimo Stilton